Emanuel and the Hanukkah Rescue

HEIDI SMITH HYDE · Illustrated by JAMEL AKIB

KAR-BEN
PUBLISHING

For my sister Karen who is always there for me – H.S.H.

For Mich, 'P' and Bean – J.A.

KAR-BEN PUBLISHING, INC.
A division of Lerner Publishing Group, Inc.
241 First Avenue North
Minneapolis, MN 55401 U.S.A.
1-800-4-KARBEN

Website address: www.karben.com

Library of Congress Cataloging-in-Publication Data

Hyde, Heidi Smith.
    Emanuel and the Hanukkah Rescue / by Heidi Smith Hyde ; illustrated by Jamel Akib.
        p.   cm.
    Summary: Nine-year-old Emanuel stows away aboard a whaling ship until the Hanukkah candles in a window light the way to bring him home.
    ISBN: 978–0–7613–6625–6 (lib. bdg. : alk. paper)
    [1. Hanukkah—Fiction. 2. Jews—United States—Fiction. 3. Whaling—Fiction.] I. Akib, Jamel, ill. II. Title.
    PZ7.H9677Em 2012
    [E]—dc23   2011029014

Manufactured in the United States of America
1 – CG – 7/15/12

*T*his story is set in New Bedford, Massachusetts, once the whaling capital of the world, where in the 18th Century a group of secret Jews emigrated from Portugal. Here in this bustling whaling village, many Jews became merchants, providing sea captains with necessary provisions such as oilskins, waterproof boots, and canvas bags.

*E*manuel Aguilar knew more about whaling than most nine-year-old boys.

His father Aaron owned a shop on the wharf, where the town's whalers purchased their supplies. Here one could find waterproof boots, compasses, and barrels to store oil. The shop also sold provisions such as molasses, potatoes, flour, and salted meat.

Each year, as many as 500 ships set sail from the bustling port of New Bedford in search of whales, whose oil was used to make candles and to light the lamps in the days before electricity.

Emanuel loved talking with the whalers. Nobody could spin a story better than Captain Henshaw, and Emanuel never tired of listening to his seafaring adventures.

"Papa, when will I be old enough to go to sea?" he asked his father each time the tall, swaggering captain finished telling about one of his encounters with the mighty whale.

"The life of a whaler is lonely and dangerous, Emanuel," his father cautioned. "Sometimes men go out and never come back. Better you should grow up to be a merchant like me."

But Emanuel didn't want to sell barrels, salted meat, and waterproof boots. He wanted to be like the mighty captain and not like his timid father.

It seemed like Papa was always afraid. The Aguilars were among the Jewish families who had left Portugal, where they had to keep their Judaism a secret. Here in New Bedford they carried their fear with them.

Every year at Hanukkah, for example, Emanuel pleaded with his father to put a whale oil menorah in the window to celebrate the Festival of Lights. But Papa always refused.

"Back in the land of my birth, it was against the law for Jews to practice their religion. Any Jew caught doing so was punished."

"This isn't Portugal, Papa. This is America! No one will put us in jail for being who we are," said Emanuel.

Emanuel couldn't understand his father's fears. He didn't understand why his family could only light Shabbat candles with the shades drawn. He didn't understand why he couldn't tell his Christian friends he was Jewish. And he didn't understand why he couldn't put a menorah in the window during the Festival of Lights.

On the first night of Hanukkah, Emanuel pleaded
with his father once again to light the menorah.
"This is the holiday to celebrate our religious freedom!"
    "Not tonight, Emanuel," said Papa, sighing.
"Perhaps tomorrow."
    On the second night, Emanuel asked again.
    "Not tonight, Emanuel," said Papa wearily. "Perhaps tomorrow."

By the seventh night, Emanuel realized that neither his father, nor their Jewish neighbors, had any intention of lighting their Hanukkah lamps.

Emanuel wanted to be more like the whalers who came into the shop—brave and strong and unafraid. Tomorrow, Captain Henshaw was venturing into the cold Atlantic to hunt whales. Emanuel decided to join him. That evening before packing his bags, he wrote his father a letter:

Dear Papa,

By the time you read this note I will be on Captain Henshaw's ship. I am not sure how long I will be gone. I need to know what it's like to be free. I hope someday you can be free, too.

Love, Emanuel

The next morning when Captain Henshaw set sail, Emanuel was hiding in a barrel in the belly of the ship. "Goodbye, father," he whispered as he sailed farther and farther from the familiar shores of New Bedford.

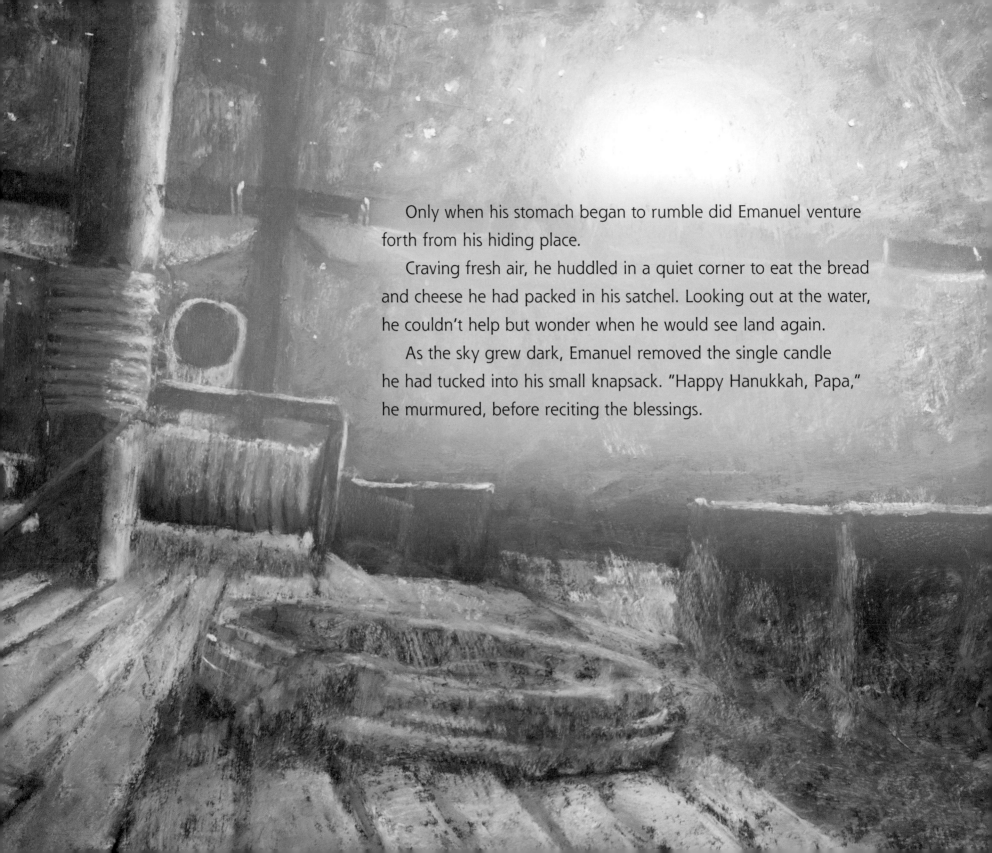

Only when his stomach began to rumble did Emanuel venture forth from his hiding place.

Craving fresh air, he huddled in a quiet corner to eat the bread and cheese he had packed in his satchel. Looking out at the water, he couldn't help but wonder when he would see land again.

As the sky grew dark, Emanuel removed the single candle he had tucked into his small knapsack. "Happy Hanukkah, Papa," he murmured, before reciting the blessings.

Suddenly the wind began to pick up, and ominous clouds rolled in. Before long, the sea began to toss the ship about.

"All hands on deck. A storm is brewing!" shouted Captain Henshaw.

Emanuel watched in horror as a giant bolt of lightning cracked the mast in two.

"We've lost the mast on the main sail," the Captain cried. "We'd best head back to New Bedford before it's too late."

The wind was blowing so hard that Emanuel
had to grab onto a rope in order to stay aboard.
"So this is what fear feels like," he thought. As he
watched the crew work tirelessly to secure the
ship, he saw a man approach. It was Jeremiah
Scott, a young blacksmith from town.

"Master Emanuel, is that you?" Jeremiah asked. "What are you doing here?"

"I snuck on board last night, and…"

"Never mind about that now. There's work to be done!
Just hold on tight while we get the ship back to port,"
Jeremiah ordered.

For hours, Captain Henshaw and his crew battled the 35-foot waves. Emanuel remembered what Papa said about whaling being lonely and dangerous. He had never felt more afraid in his entire life.

When the storm finally let up, everything became dark and still.

"Is it over, Mr. Scott? Are we almost home?" quavered Emanuel.

"Not yet. The ship has lost its bearings. The captain thinks the lighthouse was struck by lightning, and there are no stars to guide us."

Without a guiding light, the ship would surely get dashed against the rocks, Emanuel realized. Even Jeremiah Scott looked frightened.

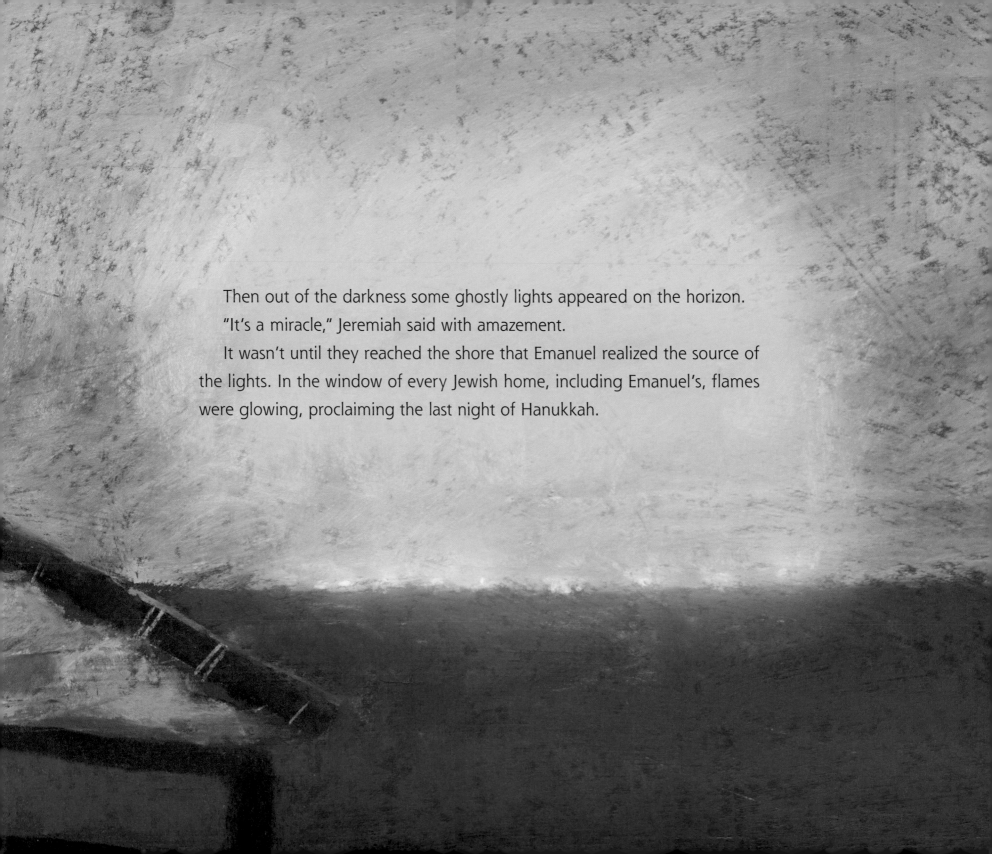

Then out of the darkness some ghostly lights appeared on the horizon.

"It's a miracle," Jeremiah said with amazement.

It wasn't until they reached the shore that Emanuel realized the source of the lights. In the window of every Jewish home, including Emanuel's, flames were glowing, proclaiming the last night of Hanukkah.

When Emanuel finally stepped off the ship, Papa was waiting. They embraced for a long time without speaking.

Finally, Emanuel said, "Papa, the oil lamps. We could see them from the ship! What happened?"

"After I read your letter I was so ashamed," Papa admitted. "I called our Jewish friends and neighbors together and convinced them to light the menorahs. You were right, Emanuel. It is not good to be ruled by fear."

"The flames helped us find our way home!" Emanuel exclaimed. "Thank you for showing us the way."

Papa smiled. "No, Emanuel. Thank you for showing me the way."

And together they returned home to celebrate the last night of Hanukkah.

About Hanukkah

Hanukkah is an eight-day Festival of Lights that celebrates the victory of the Maccabees over the mighty armies of Syrian King Antiochus. According to legend, when the Maccabees came to restore the Holy Temple in Jerusalem, they found one jug of pure oil, enough to keep the menorah lit for just one day. But a miracle happened, and the oil burned for eight days. On each night of the holiday, we add an additional candle to the menorah, exchange gifts, play the game of dreidel, and eat fried latkes and *sufganiyot* (jelly donuts) to remember this victory for religious freedom.

About the Author

HEIDI SMITH HYDE is a graduate of Brandeis University and Harvard Graduate School of Education. A former religious school teacher, she is the Director of Education of Temple Sinai in Brookline, Massachusetts. She lives in Chestnut Hill with her husband and sons. Her books include *Feivel's Flying Horses,* a National Jewish Book Award Finalist, and *Mendel's Accordion,* a Sydney Taylor Notable Children's Book and winner of the Sugarman Award for Best Jewish Children's Book.

About the Illustrator

JAMEL AKIB was born in Leigh-on-Sea, Essex, England, to mixed English and Malaysian parentage. He moved to Sabah, North Borneo, at the age of five and later returned to England to pursue his education. He has a B.A. honors degree in illustration and is an award-winning artist. Married with two children, he lives in West Sussex, England. Jamel works in chalk pastels.